A FOCUS
FOR STUDENT

As a student in the school of life I have seen many students miss their destiny because of their wrong choices of career and the wrong knowledge and mind set they have about school which has thwarted their thinking, make them think little, perform less, discover nothing, live a redundant life and lose their God given ability to fulfill destiny. The inspirational tips and nuggets of wisdom in this book help define the differences and relevance of school to life, how to prepare for life from school, it give answers to the questions you may have about school and serve as an eye opener to student, parent and individual who want to excel in school and in the school of life. There is more to school than you know!

This book possesses wisdom to help student understand the mystery of formal education and it relevance to life. It also unveils the parables of school as related to personal, societal and human development. This book is a tool for student to think properly and research what they want to do with the knowledge they acquire from school since going to school alone is not enough to make it and survive in the world we are today. So therefore, every student must be ready to discover how to use "personal education' to win their way to success in life. Why school is a book designed to prepare student for life events while in school. Issues like: What is school all about? What books are all about? Unhealthy habit that lead to failure, how to make destiny friends, how many fail in life because of school, choices and the kind of major they choose? What is failure and who is a success? Life, Wisdom, Environment and Opportunities, Character, skills, goals and employment, the after-school, pitfalls of school and proper attitude towards school and life and many more is fully dealt with in this book.

Benjamin B O
Author

Endorsements

Many people fail in life after college because they fail to answer this important question; why am I in college? The author did a good job, answering these questions. I highly recommend this book to every college freshman who is serious about success in school and in his/her professional life.

Martin Opoku-Gyamfi M.D

This is a great book. The nugget of truth presented in this book explained vividly the essence of school, book, habits, knowledge, friendship, wisdom, environment, character, opportunities, life and after-school, pitfalls of school, how to choose a major, skills, goals, employment, proper attitude toward school.

Prof Leonard Uwiringiyimana,
Pastor, Zion Temple Celebration Center-Atlanta
President, Authentic History Maker Institute
CEO, Authentic Word Ministries

This book is a good help to students and a source of motivation to students.

> Nonso Okpala Accounting Instructor
> Grambling State University

The sayings in this book are wise saying that would be used about school for years.

> Kizito Alex Student in Fort Hay University

It is a great write up, and a great book . . . .

Terwase Phd Student Grambling State University

I read the manuscript and was inspired by the wisdom in the book,

> Eazzy Noni Southeastern University LA

Great work . . . . Tunde Success, Stephen Oluwaseun, Pelumi Oluwalano Student Grambling State University

It is Inspiring. . . . Joel Opeola, Mary Olayinka. Sharon Omotor.

This is a great book. It really helps you understand the purpose of school and how it relates to life . . . .

> Angela Douglas Bsc Marketing Univeristy of Mobile Alabama, a mother of two and CEO of Angela Beauty Care

A must read for all . . . . Debroh Driggs CEO sharing&caring event planner

AuthorHouse™ LLC
1663 Liberty Drive
Bloomington, IN 47403
www.authorhouse.com
Phone: 1-800-839-8640

© 2014 by Benjamin B.O. All rights reserved.

No part of this book may be reproduced, stored in a retrieval system, or transmitted by any means without the written permission of the author.

Published by AuthorHouse   01/07/2014

ISBN: 978-1-4918-1105-4 (sc)
ISBN: 978-1-4918-1106-1 (e)

Library of Congress Control Number: 2013915734

Any people depicted in stock imagery provided by Thinkstock are models, and such images are being used for illustrative purposes only.
Certain stock imagery © Thinkstock.

This book is printed on acid-free paper.

Because of the dynamic nature of the Internet, any web addresses or links contained in this book may have changed since publication and may no longer be valid. The views expressed in this work are solely those of the author and do not necessarily reflect the views of the publisher, and the publisher hereby disclaims any responsibility for them.

Unveiling The Parables Of School

Food for thought

School is a process and not a product, a place and not a person, a means and not an end. School is a process in life with an arithmetical progression to prepare you via academic knowledge for choice making in the seas of achievement (in life). School is expected to project your talent into the seas of knowledge in order to harness success in life.

Food for thought

Your first day in school is your first day in the schooling process of life. Stay put in the process of life called school. School is a process of life not your final destination. Don't stop now go through the process!

Food for thought

The numbers you learn in school from your elementary classes speaks to you in parables of the activities in life that numbers (money making) rules in this world. So learn wisely how to count rightly now the figures that will help you figure out your destiny and time (future).

Food for thought

Languages and how to pronounce words (communicate) as being taught in school by your teacher, as a student tells you communication and networking is a key (rule) in this world. You have to know how to communicate you, your talent and ideas to be able to connect to your wealth in life as a student.

Food for thought

The quizzes, test and exams you take and go through in school speaks to you of how life is not an easy place but a place full of test and trials to get success; if you don't pass the little trials and challenges in life you can't get to your net place of success in the race to destiny.

Food for thought

School speaks to you about the process of life. The exams and quiz processes you have to go through to get to the next level in school tells you of how life is in stages and how you have to pass the challenges attached to each stages and phases of life to be able to get to the various stages and phases of life success you desire.

Food for thought

Elementary school, high school and college show you as a student how the challenges and phases of life varies, grows with time and proceeds.

Food for thought

School is a means to an end but not an end of itself, until you use it to make your ends meet. After school-life there is more to life. So be ready for life as a student.

Education is a must, school is a means, books are its requirement and learning is a continuous process in life with unending books to read. As a student education does not end in school rather it begins in school and continue all through life.

Food for thought

Going to school without a vision is like having a car without tires, going to a mall with knowing what to buy and having a body without a heart. A visionless student is a mission-less student heading to nowhere. You must have a vision for life before going to school because not knowing what to do with the knowledge acquired from school indicate not knowing what to do in life.

Food for thought

Life is a school and school is an aspect of life. Wherever you find yourself in life know you are a student (in the school of life). Life is a place of continuous learning while conclusive learning takes place in school. Keep learning every day, every time and at everywhere!

Food for thought

Learning takes place anywhere and everywhere in life. Life lessons are the common lessons you need to mix with educational knowledge to squeeze yourself into the circle of life success. Common sense is common but cannot be taught in class rather it can only be acquired via your daily dealings in the school of life mixed with calculated knowledge to survive in this world. Note, only when common sense is mixed with core knowledge that extraordinary result and success can be achieved. Keep reading, keep learning and keep living. Learning is a way of life and living is a way of learning. Whoever is not daily learning is daily dying.

Life is a mystery, school is your preparation ground for life but you are the most needed ingredient that determines your future. You are all that is needed for your destiny to come to manifestation, don't lose you (your identity)

Food for thought

School only inspires you to read while life inspires you to act, but you will become what you inspire yourself in life to read because what you read is what you will become and what you become comes as a result of what you read. Be inspired by you to read and succeed in life.

School only gives you the fact to careers but does not give you the truth on how to achieve a successful life and career. However, it takes your personal study in the path, passion and process of career you have chosen for yourself and life to produce greater success for you in life.

Food for thought

Everybody wants to be in school, but not everyone is meant to be in a School with four walls (school building). Education takes place in all places and at all times. Everywhere in the world is a school and a learning class room.

School is a waste if it cannot be used to succeed in life, education is a huge frustration without success in life. Enroll in school and be determined to use education and not to lose the education you need to personally make you a success.

Food for thought

School is a place for definite education and life is the place for continuous education. As a student of life and student in college, let your everyday living be a school and your everyday learning become your lifestyle. Learn something new every day.

Food for thought

Education is a personal responsibility; your personal responsibility to read books relevant to your destiny and figure out ways to use academic knowledge to achieve life's success. What you learn and what you know is your personal responsibility.

Food for thought

Success is driven by hard work and life is driven by success. The type of school you attend do not determine the height of success you will attain in life. Go through school and study hard. Don't do school, do hard work.

Failures are not those who fail in class rooms, rather failures are those who fail in the class room of life.

Food for thought

If you make first class in school and cannot make first class in life, then you have failed the purpose of school, education and certification. Let first class in life "be a must" and a mission to you as a student and live a first class life on earth.

If you graduate without a vision for your world, you have succeeded graduating as a blind scholar. As a certified vision-less graduate populating the blind market in the world, besides with the ongoing economic recession in the world; the world don't need more blind minds, the world need minds that can see the future and make something great out of it. You are the next Bill Gate the world need, think deep and come out with an idea that will change your world.

Food for thought

Education is a must for everyone but profitable only to those who know the benefit of studies. Do you know the benefit of education before diving into school? School comes with benefit, know the benefit and fix yourself in one (school). Let these lead you to think, re-think, search and research in order to find your purpose in life.

Food for thought

Schooling begins at home. Learning begins with your parents, and your home is your first class room, with your brothers and sisters as your (first) class mate. Parent, guidance, brothers, sisters, friends and family mind what you teach and do in the present of your student (children).

Food for thought

School is a means to an end, a means to achieve success and not a complete success as a whole. While in school know you are in the process of achieving life success. Stay put!

Food for thought

School is absolutely a societal demand but not an absolute requirement for a successful life. It takes more than school to succeed in life, go to school, be in school but in all your getting's get wisdom for life success.

Food for thought

School only teaches you how to read but does not teach you how to reach your destiny or be rich in life. Education comes with a demand; a demand for your personal effort to navigate your life into success via studies, using the knowledge you acquire from school to arrive at your destiny (future).

Education is a personal exercise not a group affair; learn to study on your own, success requires your personal investment on you and less reliance on others.

Food for thought

School only propels who you are on the inside to meet with what you want to be on the outside (in society) and only you can propel yourself to become what the world will know you for and read about you in the nearest future.

Food for thought

School set-up is not meant for everybody but only worthwhile to those who know it's worth (value). If you are not ready to comply with the process of being taught (schooled), school becomes a waste of time and a waste of investment for you.

Food for thought

School and education is not a medium of escaping poverty, rather they are medium to escape the hardship of ignorance. Go for knowledge, buy books, buy knowledge, pay for information and flee from ignorance: ignorance kills.

Food for thought

School is a means to an end not an end of itself, until you use it to make your ends meet. Is your schooling and personal education making your ends meet?

Food for thought

Books can break you, make you broke or make you a billionaire, depending on the kind of books you are reading. What kind of book is sharpening and making the path of your life and mind?

Food for thought

Your future is as big as you can see it in your mind as a student from your class room. So from class, view the future, see the blessings in life and overcome the challenges thereof from your within to your without.

Food for thought

School only gives you access to a job, but it takes you and your attitude to excel in such a job. Mind your attitude.

Food for thought

Academic certificate can only get you jobs and not promotion (a career in life and not success in life) but your character and diligence in what you do is what will sustain you, your job and promote you in life.

Food for thought

If you do not have the mind to dive into the sea of reading, do not dive into education, for education is an unending sea of books to read. Education only has a beginning but has no end. Keep learning.

Food for thought

School is not a place for professionals; it is a place where students turn their life passion into professionalism. So let your passion be your possession and your possession become your profession.

Food for thought

School is not only a building or buildings; it is a world of continuous book reading. Be a reader of life's unfolding lessons, learn as you grow, leader as you read and put to practice all profitable things you read from books, situations and from people.

Food for thought

Schooling is the beginning of class work (exercise) for life's lesson and the world is a place for hard work to make hard currency and higher class in life. Start now to learn life's lessons to harness life blessings!

Food for thought

School doesn't make you rich, it is the richness of your heart and mind that makes true riches. Enrich your mind today via books and enrich your life with healthy habit.

Food for thought

School is an integral part of life that requires your personal study, reading, researching books filled with life's wisdom to make it in life. However, the kind of books you read and the kind of books you seek wisdom from shape and determine your life, your success and future.

Food for thought

School does not make anyone rich, but continuous life education and application does make many riches. Make reading your habit and continuous reading your lifestyle. Until you reach out to study, you will not be able to reach out to riches and richness in life.

Food for thought

Education is a continuous learning and application of life's lessons but when learning's are not applied foolishness emerge. Be a doer of the right things you learn, a doer of what is right and a doer of what is wise and expedient.

Food for thought

Your wealth in education is discovering what you can do with the knowledge you acquired and the information you gather that others cannot handle (manage) like you. For in you lies unsearchable knowledge and power to change your world. Search within you now and discover the un-tapped wonders residing in you.

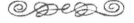

Food for thought

Your wealth in education is the worth of information in you, converted to wisdom and reproduces as a product required in life. In all your getting, get knowledge, get understanding and acquire more information for life success.

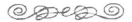

Food for thought

The numbers of knowledge daily processed by your mind via education determine the wealth and worth of your life now and in future. Think through, read through, think deep, learn wide and think thoroughly in all life situation before you act.

Food for thought

Education is discovering the knowledge of what you love to do, to change what you hate. Let education transform you and transfer productive success into your life.

Food for thought

Education makes you a problem solver, but if your education does not make you solve problems, then the essence of your education is a waste.

Food for thought

Education is for minds that are willing to change and until you experience changes in your mind; schooling, studies and teachings, become a waste.

Food for thought

Education is not for those who hate changes and learning is not for those who hate process. Learning is a process of changing mind set, and until you experience a change in your mind set, you cannot be classified as being a learned person (educated).

If education is hard work to you as a student, then try hard labor as an alternative. Learning is cheap, hard labor is expensive, go to school and get education by all means!

Food for thought

Education is student's hard work to escape life's hard labor. Be in school, study hard and be focused in life.

Food for thought

School is a place for mental training (development) but if school is not mentally training (challenging) you to change and advance in your thinking, then the essence of school become a waste to you.

Food for thought

School is a place for mental training (development), while life is the place to experiment WHAT YOU HAVE LEARNED IN SCHOOL; a place to weigh and process your mental capacity to solve life's challenges and make success.

School is a place where academic failures may be allowed, while life is a place where failure is not permitted nor meant to be tried. The world applauds only success and detests failure. Success rules in life refuse failure today!

Food for thought

It is better to fail in school than to fail in life, because failure in life will be failure in your destiny, career and purpose but whenever you fail in life let your failure ignite your passion for succeed by using the injuries of your failure as injector to project you to success in life. However, in life be prepared for both success and failure but always strive to avoid failure because failure comes with a lot of bitterness, injuries and shame.

Failure is an attempt not a person, whenever you experience failure in anything you do, know it is an attempt made by you that failed, not you for you are better off in many other events you are yet to attempt. An event you attempt may fail but in you are many other successful events yet to be attempted that will succeed. You are not a failure in life; make a difference, attempt something different that may lead you to your success after you must have failed in other event.

Food for thought

School is a place for students with visions and not a playing ground for all and sunder. Student with no vision and ambition should not be found in school. When you have no vision as a student, you have no future, and have no need to waste your time in school. Be a student with a vision and mission for the world.

Food for thought

School is a place for minds with a mission in life; it is not a place for minds filled with emptiness concerning the issues of life. To succeed in life you need to personally focus your mind to study, eradicate all junks off your mind, discuss success and not gossip, get a mission and a vision for your life.

Food for thought

School is a place for minds that are ready to change their world and make their world a better place, not for minds that are anti-change to changes that will change their life for the better. If you are not ready for changes don't bother yourself going to school.

Food for thought

School is a place for personality discovery; a place where 'who you are' on the inside is being processed with academic drills to meet life's demands.

Food for thought

School is a place where you acquire your first mental strength; a place where your weakness is tested and your strengths are discovered while life is a place where your weaknesses are not tolerated to attain and compete for success.

Food for thought

School is a place where your weaknesses should be converted into strength, and where your strengths should be turned into fulfillment.

Food for thought

School is a breeding ground and not a playing ground, it is a place you convert your dreams into reality and your realities to achievement.

Food for thought

Certificate and being in school is not a guarantee for life success. If you depend on school alone for life success, you may be disappointed. Solemnly dependence on certificate gotten from school may lead to frustration but when you certify and fortify your mind with knowledge that will articulate your success in life, your success will have no limit.

Food for thought

Your future as a student does not depend on school alone; rather it depends on how you can use academic work to see and set your future aright. As a student see the future through books and catch the lessons of life via learning. Be a student of life.

Food for thought

The greatest education you need to acquire in the journey of life are; the knowledge of how to manage time, resource and people. These three essential elements are the factors that will connect you to success and uplift you to the top in life. Stay connected to time, manage your resource and don't lose the people you need to get to the top in life.

Food for thought

School is a place where your career initiation begins: a place where your life's dreams can be nursed to maturity using academic exercise combine with COMMON SENSE in order to meet the demand of the world for success.

Food for thought

School is a place for personality discovery: a place where you discover, create and choose your own personality design (style/brand) for life, and a place where you create your own market (brand) for the world at large.

Food for thought

School is a place where life time friends are made: Friends that can frame (support) you into your destiny and friends that can freeze you from your destiny. Be careful the kinds of friends you make in school.

Food for thought

School is a place for life's disciplines; the discipline of reading, passing exams, and making effort towards success which is equally the same discipline required for success in life. If you are not ready for discipline have no need to be in school.

Food for thought

School is a place you make network (you make lifetime network); important life networks required for the future. As a student you are not just in school to study; you are in school to network your life to success. While in school take advantage of the network. Ultimately, from school learn to make lifetime network that will connect your now to the future. Start making the future connections you need now as student.

Food for thought

School is the first connecting point of a child to the outside world. It is student first meeting point with the world after home; for the life of all students start from home to school and from school to the world. Stay connected!

Food for thought

School connects your present to your future and your future to the features you personally focus your mind on while in the class.

Food for thought

School is a projector; a projector that either projects you to the world, or prolong your days in the room of education, depending on how you use the knowledge, time and information you acquire from school.

Food for thought

School is the place you start learning life's disciplines; from the discipline of how to keep to time, to the discipline of searching and studying things required for life.

Food for thought

School is not all about class room exercise; it is a class with the world as its perimeter, and the world as its study material. Study beyond the limit of school.

Food for thought

The world does not need your certificate after school rather the world only needs your certified ideas after graduation to make ends meet both for you and for others.

Food for thought

School is a channel and an incubating womb through which students can reach their goal in life. If you want to reach your goal in life, stay through the process of school and life.

Food for thought

The world wants (seek) the best of you and not the worst of you, but it takes schooling yourself with books that contain the essential knowledge required for the future and your success to be a success in life.

Graduating from school does not guarantee you a job or a better life after school rather it ground you if you do not have a grand vision and a grand mission for life before graduation.

Food for thought

School does not solemnly determine your future; your future is determined by the quality of education you personally feed your mind.

If you don't know how to value and manage people, you will not be able to emerge into life's successes and get to the top in life. For people are the connecting factor you need to function in your future. Value people and manage people you meet in life.

Food for thought

You are the only one with the right to your dreams and visions, refuse all negative voices that may be speaking against you and your vision. Refuse all things that may want to stop your future and success in life.

Food for thought

From school, a good student sees the possibilities out there in the world and covert the hurdles of education to meet the potential riches awaiting them in the world after school.

Food for thought

You can never excel in the field of study you don't love. Your strength lies in what you love. What you love is the potential power to your success in life. In what you love is your wisdom and power to rule your world. Read what you love to study, love what you read and read what you love to excel in!

Food for thought

The subject in school that you love is the potential power for your success and wisdom in life. As you identify those subjects you identify the power you need to excel in life.

Food for thought

School is not for minds that worry about the unnecessary issues of life; it is for students whose passion is to change the worries of life into wealth. What are you worried about as a student?

Food for thought

If you graduate without a solid mission for your future, you have just succeeded graduating as an additional mess to the world.

Food for thought

School is for opened minds, ready to be filled with new ideas. Learn something new every day as a student and fill your mind with good ideas!

Food for thought

An open mind goes to school to see and catch life's lights and vision but if your mind is filled with the full knowledge and wisdom you need for your life before school, then going to school is not a mandatory for you (you don't need school), rather all you need is an avenue for manifestation. School is not for all and not all you need to succeed in life. Wisdom is all and all you need in life. Get wisdom!

Food for thought

Every student is like a blank board going to school to be filled with life's facts and ideas. As student you must go to school with an open mind to receive optima ideas that will make a difference to you and the world at large.

Food for thought

Until you discover in school the visions and missions for your life, only then can you discover your space and place in life; then only can the essence of school be counted as a gain and not as a waste of time, resource and life to you.

Food for thought

No one is born with knowledge, school is not the home of life's knowledge rather school is a place where knowledge can be acquired and life is a place where practical knowledge is learned and displayed. Enroll in school, pay for knowledge and acquire wisdom for life's success.

Education is a good investment to those who know how to reap its reward and a bad investment to those who do not know how to reap the benefit. If you do not know the value of education, you can't reap the reward of education. It will be foolishness to invest in what will not profit you, the resources you need to acquire knowledge in other trade you may be good at doing. Do not be deceived, not all those who go to school make it in life and not many others who do not go to school don't also make it in life but only those who knows how to personally educate themselves for life success make it every time in life. Decide today and define today what is good for you and don't let norms or societal culture dictate the path of your life career for you.

Food for thought

School is an integral part of life that is required to prepare you for the greater part of your future. While in school make preparation via studies for the greater part of your life.

Food for thought

School is an incubating womb for destiny; a channel through which destiny processes can be learned. School is not the future but a means to prepare for the future. Go to school, go through the process of school and take advantage of the access and assets school has in stock for your future.

Food for thought

What is education? Education is feeding your mind with all healthy edible knowledge that can cater and improve your life for the better. Be educated, stay educated and be informed.

Food for thought

Education is a life time investment and a gold mine but until you invest into the gold mine of education, the world will not mine you. When you mine education, then will the world mind you (your works). Mind you, in life you must study to show yourself approved and qualify for the wealth in the world to be yours!

Food for thought

Students who cannot adhere to principles of school lack the potential to follow through the principles and process of success in life. As a student be law abiding, be above the law by keeping and living beyond the edges of the law.

Food for thought

The future only belongs to those who can see possibilities from within, using knowledge acquired from books, school and teachings to discern and navigate their destiny. See the future in you, read the future ahead and start living the future from now!

Success is when preparation meets productive opportunity in life. As a student let your preparation be open to opportunity and your opportunity be converted to productive success. Be open to opportunities, be prepared for success and don't let opportunities elude you in life.

Success is a continuous stage in life and not a bus stop (in the process of life). However, your present success in life is a stepping stone to your next success or phase of success in life. Don't stop now on your present success, keep moving because your present success is the ladder to your next success and your next success is the beginning of all others successes to come.

Food for thought

Success never fights changes rather success embraces changes (challenges and success flock together). Every change in life imposes a challenge and all challenges are rooted for success. Be an agent of change. Be the change your world need.

Food for thought

Success never runs away from challenges, rather success turns challenges to championship stories. Covert your challenges to success, your success to stories and your stories to solution. Be success oriented and be a problem solver.

Food for thought

Success stories are filled with both wanted stones and unwanted stones. In whatever stages of success process you find yourself, you will always find challenges trying to stop you but never you give up, follow through the up and down in the race for success in life to succeed.

Books are meant for those who have booked (signed) to succeed in life. Failure is a name for those who have turn their back on studies (books) and wisdom. If you are ready to succeed in life buy books, get wisdom and read every day.

Food for thought

Books are not for the lazy, they are only for those who are ready to read; for those who are ready to turn their back on present distractions to figure out their future destination. Are you ready to figure out the future? Read books, get information.

Food for thought

Books are not for broke minds, rather they are for minds that are ready to break the walls of ignorance and enrich their lives with the wealth in education. Break the walls of ignorance, read books, acquire information, go to school and be educated.

Food for thought

Books are not for those without focus, rather they are for those who are ready to focus their minds to study and acquire life's knowledge, wisdom and success. Be focus!

Books are not for the passive, but are for the passionate whose readiness and interest is in breaking limitations, and setting new life's standard. Be active and not passive about reading, for only via reading can ignorance and poverty be extinguished.

Food for thought

Books are not for those who are not ready to search for life's knowledge to enrich and bless themselves and others. Rather books are for those who are ready to search the unsearchable seas of knowledge life have in stock for them.

Food for thought

School doesn't make you a success in life rather it is the character you cultivate both in school and in life that makes you a success or a failure in life.

Food for thought

School is a place of discovery not a place of destination for the lazy (lazy minds beware). Until you discover your future while in school you cannot be counted and seen as being relevant in the world.

Food for thought

School is a place of discovery. A place to discover who you are and what you have to offer to the world.

Food for thought

While in school see like the eagle and prepare for life like the navy seal because school is a place to experiment life's situations ahead of time (ahead of the future or future event). Be prepared for life via school.

Food for thought

School is the place where students master life situations, realities and train via educational progression for the challenges of life. Master the mystery of life via education.

Food for thought

School is a place where those who want to be tutored, tailored, and trained into the system of life's success train. If you are not ready for training, don't be found in the confines of college or school.

Food for thought

School is a place for world changers not a place for world wasters. If you want to change your world? Go for education. Be enrolled in school, be in school, be useful, and be a world changer and not a waster.

Food for thought

A wasted life is the product of an unhealthy habit. Unhealthy habit is the grave for early death. Keep yourself away from unhealthy habit. Beware of what you do, don't waste your life via unhealthy habits rather train your habit for what is right. Use your life wisely.

Food for thought

If you are not schooled, you will be screened (eliminated) from the school of success in life but when you fully school yourself with the wisdom of life the world will make you a citadel of success. As a student, personally educate and equip yourself with wisdom needed to save you from crashing in the journey of life.

Food for thought

Life will reward you with what you invest into it, while education will reward you with the same effort you put into studies. In the same vein, your life will give you, bring to you and reward you with the same attitude you invest in yourself.

Food for thought

Life reacts to you the way you respond to it, while challenges change you the way you chose to react to its demands. In life, be prepared for challenges and react to life situations wisely.

Food for thought

School changes the way you look, but if your looks still remain the same after school then you have not been schooled.

Food for thought

Prolonged education is not meant for everyone, but prolong schooling is meant for those who need prolonged teaching to master the ways of their life's successes.

Food for thought

School is a place of enlightenment, not a place of extravagant enjoyment. As a student of life you must not allow the extra-curricular activities of school distract you from your academic lessons, extra moral lessons and success in life.

Food for thought

School is a place of inspiration not a place of relaxation. So don't relax or relent on your educational activities.

Food for thought

School is a place of preparation, not a place for lustful pleasure.

Food for thought

School is a place for hard work not a place for bad gang.

Food for thought

School is a place for goal getters not a place for jokers.

Food for thought

School is a place where ambition is birth, not a place where ambition resides.

Food for thought

School environment is a place where baby (pre-matured) minds grow into maturity, not a place where baby (pre-mature) minds are not willing to grow over life's issues and situation. Note: When you come to school with an innocent mind it is expected of you to graduate with a mature mind ready for life.

Food for thought

If you graduate with a babyish/puerile mind from school, then you have succeeded in graduating as a failure: one who is not ready for life.

Food for thought

Real life successes are not for babies, rather they are for minds that are ready to be in control of life's situations and lessons via learning.

Food for thought

School is the place where great minds are molded into desired shape, while life is the place where great mind users graduate their knowledge into life's success.

Food for thought

School is not a place for lazy minds but a place where young minds are activated and shaped into desired societal shapes and sizes of success via hard work.

Food for thought

Schooling is hard work, if it is not hard to you, try taking some exams and make all A's.

Food for thought

School is a place where kings are made not a place where kings are born. Nobody in school is better than you; it is just the extra effort (mile) they put into their academic work than you that make them seems better. Go extra-mile and become an extraordinary king on earth.

Food for thought

Kingship mind-set is a requirement for education while kingship life style is lived outside of school via educational process. Don't feel like a king while you are still in school because kings live outside school via successful ideas.

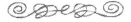

Food for thought

School is a place where soldiers of life success are made, not a place for students who are not ready to fight for life's success. As a student be prepared to fight your success in life!

Food for thought

School is a preliminary battle field to battle your space in the circle of life's success. However, most success in life requires you to practice in school what you want to put into practice in life. What have you conceived as a student in class while in school to show to the world as a product of your studies and discovery?

Food for thought

Life is a battle ground for success and without battling; you can't have your portion in the field of success in life.

Food for thought

Life is a place for student to live the dreams that they conceive in their mind while in school, not a place for students who lack the aspiration to become somebody in life. Life is a place for serious business, be serious with your life!

Food for thought

Life is a place you execute dreams conceived in school, while school is a place where dreams are conceived.

Food for thought

Life is not a place for minds that are not ready to learn through the processes of life, but a place for minds ready for daily education in the school of life's situations and happenings.

Food for thought

Life is a school, while school is a path of life. School is a path of life while life is an unending schooling process.

Food for thought

School is a place of continuous trial; a place where you try again and again until you pass, that is why school is spelt with double O's. If you fail in an event in school or life, do not give up. Try again and again until you excel in the same event or in another attempt of a different event. Life and school have unlimited chances (attempt) for you to prove your success (that you are not a failure). Keep trying don't stop trying until you succeed.

Food for thought

School is a place to rehearse the plans you have to liaise (bargain) with life. However, to succeed in life liaise (bargain) your way to success via personal schooling of your passion, ways and ideas to success while in school.

Food for thought

School is for a definite time not forever and it is an integral part of your days in life. Spend your days in school wisely so you do not waste your days in life in misery pursuing educational degree.

Food for thought

School is the place where great minds are built while life is the place where great minds manifest their greatness. Build in school whatever you want to manifest in life. Ensure you have something to manifest to your world as a student?

Food for thought

School is a place of decision while Life is a place of your manifestation. As a student start deciding now the decision that best manifest your success in life.

Food for thought

School is your first network ground. Life is your net exploit ground. As a student make godly (legal) exploit with the knowledge you acquire from school in life.

Food for thought

Who you are in school is not who you are in life, because real life and school life are two different entities and experiences. Whoever fails in school and succeeds in life is a true success, he or she is better than those who passed college but failed in life. True success is seen or achieved in life not in school. Academic Knowledge alone cannot determine your life success and destiny.

Food for thought

Who you will become in life depends on what you have chosen to do with what you have learned in school. Whatever you learn in school is a driving force for your destiny and life. What are you learning in school and how is school lining up your life and mind?

Food for thought

How you portray yourself in school is a reflection of how you have seen, measured and valued your future to be; because the way you position yourself in your mind determines the position you occupy in life. See the greatness inside of you while in school.

Food for thought

You are a brand in school waiting for life opportunity to explode. So watch out and never let opportunities pass you by.

Food for thought

WHO ARE YOUR FRIENDS WHILE IN SCHOOL? Because your friends while in school determine the strength, the knowledge and height you will attain now in school and in the future.

Food for thought

READING AND STUDYING: there is a big difference between reading and studying. You read to pass exams in school as a student, but study to pass the exams of both school and life.

Food for thought

As a student, you pass school exams for what purpose? To succeed in life or to be a champion in school: Success bound students' read to pass both school exams and life's challenges.

Food for thought

THINKERS AND TAKERS; there is a big difference between a thinker and a taker and a big difference between schooling and being educated. Education makes you a thinker, while your personal audacity makes you a taker; someone who jumps and takes advantage of life's opportunities and convert it to wealth via effective education.

Food for thought

A graduate is a student with an upgraded mind and an upgraded thinking faculty. A student who thinks through the process of school, assimilate life knowledge, educate his or her mind, and take advantage of the best opportunities in life are called graduate (not student who refuse to think through life via education). Think via education, take step via wisdom and take complete control over life's opportunities.

Food for thought

There are two kinds of students in school: students who want to pass the exams of school and others that want to pass the exams of life. Those who want to pass the exams of school do not worry themselves preparing for life; while student who want to pass the exam of life position themselves to pass the exams of school and the exam of life.

TEACHING AND LEARNING: There is a difference between teaching and learning. Teaching comes from what you are taught, while learning comes from what you decide to study and to know for your personal use both to pass exams and to succeed in life.

Food for thought

AFTER GRADUATION WHAT NEXT?

After graduation you either create a job or seek for a job. You create jobs using the knowledge you acquire from school to ignite ideas capable of becoming a company and suitable to hire you and others. Only then have you fulfill the purpose of certification. School certified you as a graduate; a person capable of handling life challenges, job challenges, and unemployment challenges, to fall short of these qualities is to fail the course that has certified you as a graduate (school). In life, only a few intelligent students after graduation use the knowledge they acquired from school (that graduated from within them) to create jobs suitable for the kind of lifestyle and passion they want. While other (student) lay back student pursue jobs thus become a used and lose tool for the owners of the company they work for, instead of them becoming a tool to their own life success rather they become a tool to be use and be useless. Job seekers are hired modern slaves to their bosses because more often than not, they are not free, they don't leave a free life, they live for their boss, they are always bound by the jobs and by the company that hire them and their wages and salaries cannot be equated with the knowledge and strength they have inputted into the company that hired them. When other graduates that create jobs for themselves fully utilize the knowledge they acquired from school to create lasting success and lasting income for themselves. Note, it is the knowledge you acquired from school that makes you a graduate; qualified for life's challenges and a creator of jobs. Be a graduate with great ideas. Let ideas graduate with you as you enter into the world market as a graduate. Create ideas that will change your life and the world forever.

Food for thought

School is a place to learn from others. Don't be an island while in school.

WHAT GRADUATES IN YOU AND OUT OF YOU?

(Q: As a graduate what graduate from your within to your without):

As a graduate ideas and knowledge should graduate with you from college to indicate the changes and advancement that has taken place in your mind. At the same time, some amount of ignorance should have been expelled from you as a sign of being educated. Ideas and creative ability ought to graduate from within you as a graduate, to create opportunities for you and others as a tangible evidence for the world to know of a truth you earn and not pay for your degree.

Food for thought

WHAT DOES SCHOOL MEAN TO YOU? Whatever school means to you is what you will get out of school and until you define what school is to you; you will never be able to define and find your future and success via education in life (education will not be useful or necessary to you in life).

Food for thought

SCHOOL IS A PLACE OF CHOICE.

From school you make choices that will choke you or change you. The choices you make while in school create the chances you meet in life as a graduate. School is a place where your life choices can be harness for life success and opportunities.

Food for thought

School opens your mind to new ideas but life opens your mind (life) to new challenges. As a student you have to open your mind while in school and prepare for the challenges in life before graduation.

Food for thought

While in school, listen with your ears and hear with your heart how to harness the educational arithmetic in school to mathematically create your life's achievement.

Food for thought

WHY THIS MAJOR?

Your choice of major is your choice of the kind of life you want to live and the choice of your life time career. Don't let your choice be propelled by others rather let your major be propelled by what you want to major in life (specialize in).

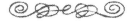

Food for thought

Don't choose a major for a career which you don't have passion for, because what you don't have passion for, you cannot pass the challenges it has awaiting you in life.

Food for thought

There is a big difference between achievement and fulfillment. Achievement does not have lasting peace and joy while fulfillment does. Fulfillment is the manifestation of your life vision, mission and purpose covered with lasting joy, peace and lot of achievement in stock. Note; not all achievers are fulfilled in life but all fulfiller are achievers.

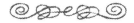

WHAT ARE YOU LEARNING IN SCHOOL?

You learn knowledge IN SCHOOL, learn friendship and earn success IN LIFE. These three elements are the required possession you need to acquire and earn while in school. You learn how to know what to do in life, learn how to choose the friends to sail and network your knowledge in life to success with, and pursue how to earn your place (success) in life.

Food for thought

KNOW THE REQUIRED SKILLS FOR YOUR MAJOR AND ACQUIRE THEM

Only fools dive into a course without finding out the cost of such a course. Don't be a graduate in a major without knowing and acquiring the required skills for such a career (major) in life. Get the skills and not the school! So many students are full of school and not the skills required for them to function after school.

Food for thought

The word entrepreneur can be broken down into: enter = what enters into your mind. preneur what you premeditate and interpret to produce a (new idea/product) Neur = new idea. Be an entrepreneur at all times in life.

Food for thought

INTELLIGENT AND BRILLIANT STUDENT there is a big difference between an intelligent student and a brilliant student. Intelligent students prepare from school to pass life's exam(to overcome the challenges in life) through school exams (assessment), while brilliant students are students who are stereotype in all they do (they do just school and abstain themselves from other societal activities needed to fix them into the society); they only prepare to pass school exams without preparing for challenges ahead in life; they study to pass school exams only without preparing themselves to pass and overcome life challenges(their future life situation). Be in school, be an intelligent student and prepare for life from school.

Food for thought

DREAMERS AND LOSERS IN SCHOOL

School is a place where you find these two students (a dreamer and a looser) in the same class; you will find in school few students catch dreams for their life and many others losing the dreams for their life. Are you losing your dreams in school or acquiring more dreams for life?

VISIONARY AND VISITORS IN SCHOOL

School is the place where you find a visionary and a visitor in the same place (class). A place where some students make themselves visitors in school; these categories of students come to school but are never involved with the academic process of being in school. They go to school just for the fun of it (to have the fun), they are careless about the academic activities in school, while the visionary students see the future through school and catch a successful life vision.

Food for thought

JOB SEEKERS AND JOB CREATORS

There are two kinds of students that graduate from school; the job seekers and the job makers. As a student where do you belong? Is your education making you create jobs or seek for jobs? Job seekers beg for space in life while job creators take their space in life through calculated invention and ideas that create job for them and others.

LABOUR MARKET

School is a market that prepares you for labor (labor market), while life is a market where only the wise wins by personal discovery (education) that projected them to success using ideas acquired from school to escape the hardness in the world labor market.

APPLICANT AND APPLIERS (IDEAS LEARNED IN SCHOOL)

There are two students in school and there are two kinds of students that graduate from school; a handful graduate as applicant who seeks favor from others to be used (employed), while the others graduate as applier; one who apply the knowledge acquired and learned in class to make their ends meet and create successful jobs for others in life. What kind of a student are you? An applicant or an applier.

Food for thought

SET GOALS

School is a place to set your goals for life's roles. Intelligent student from school set their goals and map out their way for success. Start now to set your life goals from school.

ACHIEVE YOUR GOALS

As a student, never allow anybody to stop you from achieving your goals, from school start cultivating ideas that will rule your world because in the world only ideas rules and calculated preparation give birth to life successful manifestation.

Food for thought

EARLY RETIREMENT

In life never you set your mind to work for someone for more than the days you spend in college because if you do, you've succeeded wasting your life and education in building other people's dreams, for the number of years you spend in college is the required number of years you need to get yourself ready, trained and set for your own business or idea (if you were unable to start up yours after graduation). Note it may be good to work for someone after graduation, but it is expedient to do so for a while and then pull out to start your own business or company in order to fulfill your own life dreams and destiny. Think about this, if your dad and my dad started their own company and firm, there would have been a lot of jobs available today and we would have no need to go looking for a job out there as a graduate.

SOLVE PROBLEMS

School is a place where problem solvers think through life problems and solve it all via calculated academic proceeds and thinking. However, school should be a place where student are to be made to solve life problems and not a place where student are graduated to become more problem to the world. Is your education making you a problem solver or a problem maker?

Food for thought

Your prosperity lies in your problem. The more problems you solve the more you prosper. Don't run away from problems for problems are your projector for prosperity.

Food for thought

Everyone on earth is a lifelong student; a student of life's experiences and situations. Whatever you go through as a student know you are coming out with a lesson and ideas that will rule your world. As long as you live you can't avoid life lessons and learnings.

Food for thought

Complain make your life complex. Compliance make your life complete. Stop complaining and start complying with the wisdom that will make your life a success. Read books. Read books that are relevant to your life.

Why school? If school is what they say it is, why are there so many poor educated people even professors waiting for the government to spoon fed them after graduating from college? Why is it that they are so many educated people today than before and still the world is experience more crises and depression, recession like never before. School only cannot help you succeed in life rather it is only the system you personally carve out for yourself that will bring success to you in life. School is not all you need in life to succeed; all you need is wisdom. Wisdom from above that is above ordinary human reasoning is all you need to make good success in life.

Food for thought

As a student of life, love school, go to school, catch a dream, dream a dream and achieve your dreams, goals and objectives for your life. Education is a must and you are the needed material the world is waiting for to manifest!

About the author

Benjamin Babawale Oluwole

I believe there are no failures in life, things fail not you. You are made by God and all you need in life has been given and deposited in you by God. Your potentials all reside inside of you, all you need to do is to look inside of you and discover the treasure within and use it all to make the world a better place.

Benjamin B.O.

Am from a family of eight; got my first degree from OOSU, second degree from LCP and third degree from GSU USA. Nevertheless, I am still in the school of life and of the Holy God. I give all the glory to God, thanks to my pastors, prophet, family, friends and fans for all their support. I give reference to all my teachers, the bible and the uncountable books have read, the experiences have gone through in life that has taught me the pattern and path of life written in this book.

However, the sayings in this book came from my life experiences in school and from my daily inspirational meditation inspired by God and life situations. I recommend this book for every student, parent and individual who wants to excel in life. This book is loaded with wisdom for life.